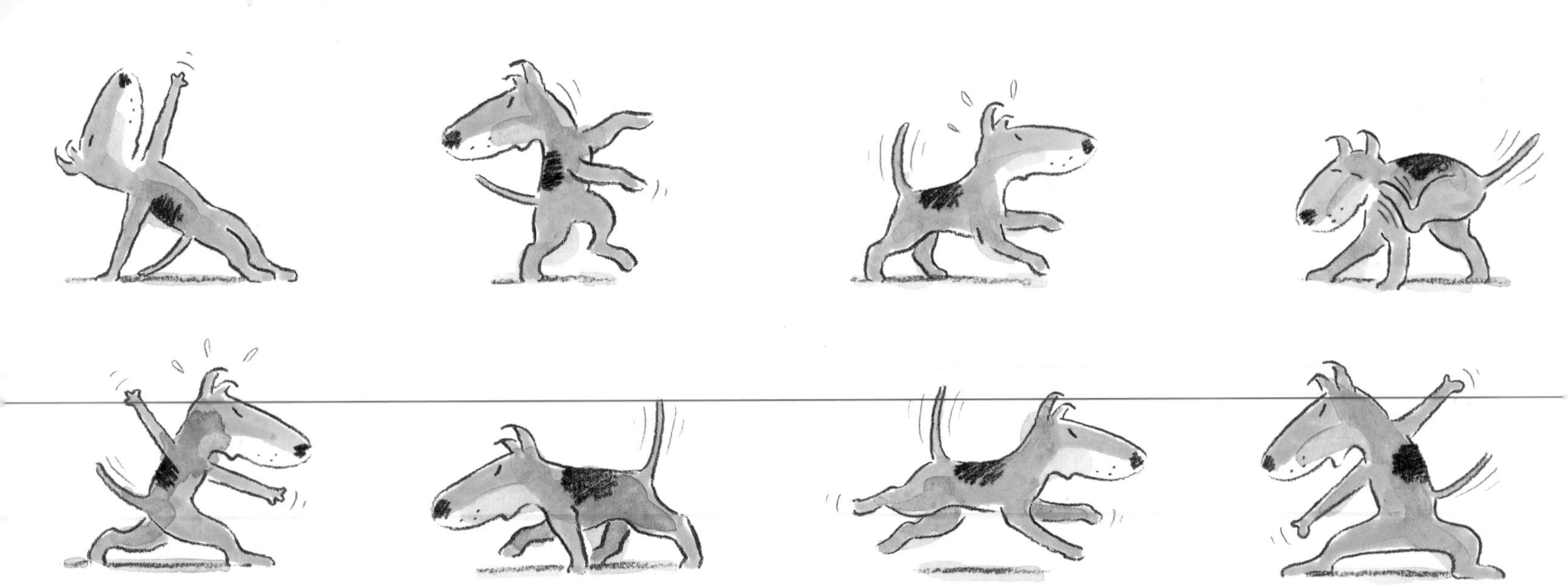

This book belongs to:

For Pauline Lock F.S.

For Ying Liu J.L.

First published in Great Britain in 2003
by Orion Children's Books
This edition published 2004 by Dolphin Paperbacks
a division of the Orion Publishing Group Ltd
Orion House
5 Upper St Martin's Lane
London WC2H 9EA

A catalogue record for this book is available from the British Library.

Printed in Italy
ISBN 1 84255 243 0

LITTLE YELLOW DOG

GETS A SHOCK

WORDS BY FRANCESCA SIMON · PICTURES BY JAMES LUCAS

Dolphin

Little Yellow Dog trotted into the sitting room.

WHOOPEE!

This was his lucky day.
The chair was empty.

Ginger Cat was licking her paws by the window.

'Hi, Ginger Cat,'

said Little Yellow Dog.

'Hi, Little Yellow Dog,'

said Ginger Cat.

'Time for my nap,' said Little Yellow Dog.

He leapt into the chair.

So did Ginger Cat.

'Hey. Off!'

said Little Yellow Dog.

'I got here first,'

said Ginger Cat.

said Little Yellow Dog.

'No! Mine!'

'This chair isn't big enough for both of us,'

growled Little Yellow Dog.

'Hoo right. Get off,'

hissed Ginger Cat, giving
him a great big push.

'How did I end up on the floor?'
said Little Yellow Dog.

Little Yellow Dog had an idea.

He crept up to the chair . . .

. . . sneaked behind . . .

and . . .

'RAAAAAA!'

shrieked Little Yellow Dog

Ginger Cat went flying.

'Look out...

...it's the monster!'

yelled Little Yellow Dog.

'And...he's...coming...

...to...get...you!'

On and on and on they ran, until they were too tired to run any more.

'Friends?'
said Little Yellow Dog.

'Friends,'
said Ginger Cat.

'We can share the chair,' said Little Yellow Dog.

'Of course we can,' said Ginger Cat.

But when they saw the chair,
they got a shock.

Bad Rabbit was there!

'Oi, get off our chair!'
said Little Yellow Dog and Ginger Cat.

'It's a shared chair,' said Bad Rabbit.

'Snuggle up!'

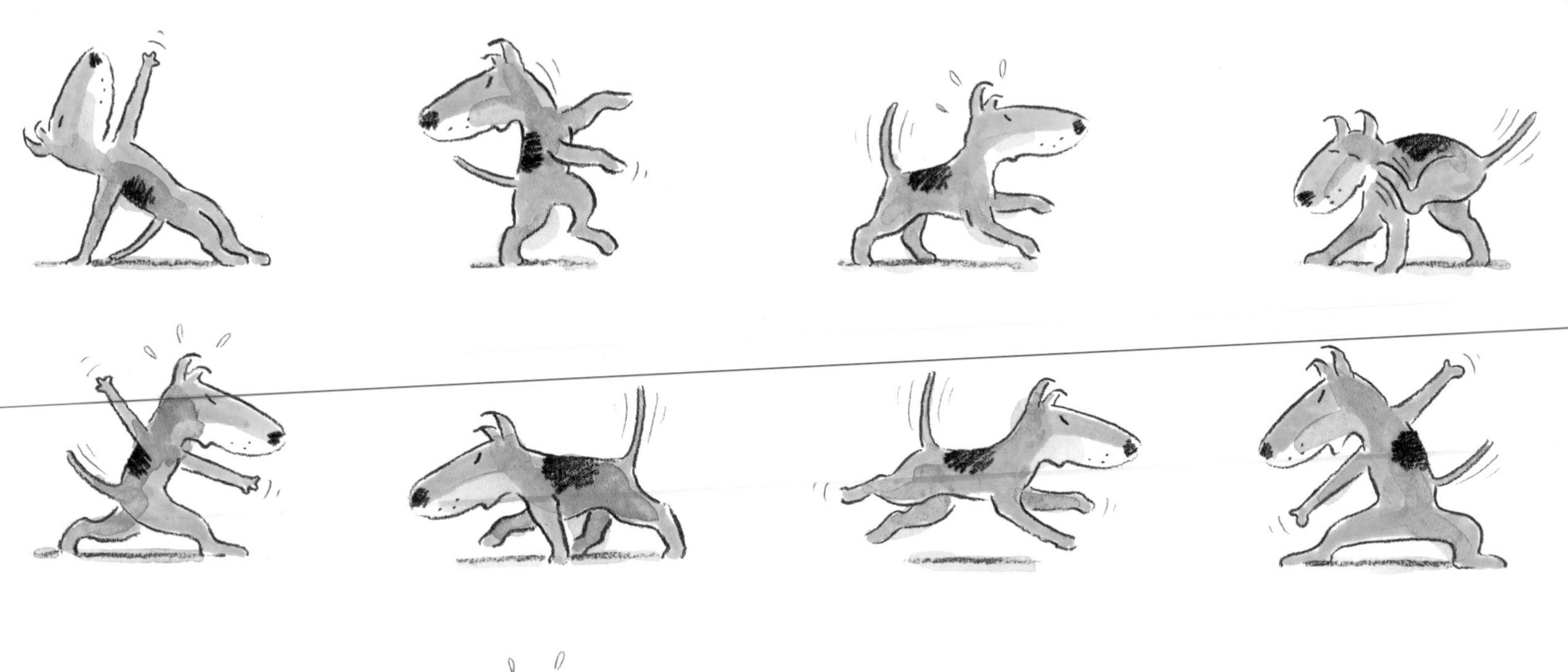